HOW TO DEAL

COPING WITH LOSS AND GRIEF

MICHELLE GARCIA ANDERSEN

Rourke Educational Media

A Division of Carson Dellosa Education

rourkeeducationalmedia.com

ROURKE'S SCHOOL to HOME CONNECTIONS
BEFORE AND DURING READING ACTIVITIES

Before Reading: *Building Background Knowledge and Vocabulary*

Building background knowledge can help children process new information and build upon what they already know. Before reading a book, it is important to tap into what children already know about the topic. This will help them develop their vocabulary and increase their reading comprehension.

Questions and Activities to Build Background Knowledge:

1. Look at the front cover of the book and read the title. What do you think this book will be about?
2. What do you already know about this topic?
3. Take a book walk and skim the pages. Look at the table of contents, photographs, captions, and bold words. Did these text features give you any information or predictions about what you will read in this book?

Vocabulary: *Vocabulary Is Key to Reading Comprehension*

Use the following directions to prompt a conversation about each word.
- Read the vocabulary words.
- What comes to mind when you see each word?
- What do you think each word means?

Vocabulary Words:
- denial
- depression
- fatigue
- furious
- intrusive
- memorialize
- momentous
- resentment
- rituals
- somber
- susceptible
- traumatic

During Reading: *Reading for Meaning and Understanding*

To achieve deep comprehension of a book, children are encouraged to use close reading strategies. During reading, it is important to have children stop and make connections. These connections result in deeper analysis and understanding of a book.

 ## Close Reading a Text

During reading, have children stop and talk about the following:
- Any confusing parts
- Any unknown words
- Text to text, text to self, text to world connections
- The main idea in each chapter or heading

Encourage children to use context clues to determine the meaning of any unknown words. These strategies will help children learn to analyze the text more thoroughly as they read.

When you are finished reading this book, turn to page 46 for **Text-Dependent Questions** and an **Extension Activity**.

TABLE OF CONTENTS

Defining Loss and Grief............................4
Physical Side Effects.............................10
Common Reactions 18
Grief Rituals....................................26
Looking Ahead 32
Helping Someone Who Is Grieving................38
Activity..44
Glossary.......................................45
Index 46
Text-Dependent Questions.......................46
Extension Activity 46
Bibliography....................................47
About the Author................................48

CHAPTER 1

DEFINING LOSS AND GRIEF

Daniel was at school when his grandmother passed away. She had moved in with his family when she got sick a few months before. Even though she was in pain, Daniel's grandmother always made him smile with her hugs and silly jokes. Daniel loved his grandmother very much.

When his parents told him she had died, Daniel was overwhelmed with sadness. But he also felt relief. It was hard for him to see her in pain every day. His feelings confused him. He didn't want to talk to his parents about it because he felt guilty for experiencing so many emotions at once.

When we lose someone or something we care about, we experience feelings of loss and grief. A loss can mean the death of a family member, a friend, or a pet. We also experience loss when our lives change because of events such as divorce, a friendship ending, or changes with our health. The way you respond to a loss is the way you grieve. There is no right way to grieve.

Grieving is a personal experience. When we grieve, we encounter a wide range of thoughts, emotions, and behaviors—and sometimes this can be confusing. When someone you love has been ill for some time, it is not uncommon to feel a sense of relief when they pass. It is difficult to see someone we love in pain, and it is natural to not want that person to suffer any longer. You should never be ashamed of your feelings.

Everyone experiences loss at some point in life. At these times, it's important to seek help from someone you trust or from a professional. Having someone to talk to and lean on for support can significantly help the healing process. While you are grieving, it is okay to cry, to laugh, to be alone for a while, or to spend time with others. It is okay to do whatever you need to do from moment to moment and from day to day.

Words to Know

grief – the way we think and feel in response to a loss

deceased – no longer living

bereaved – greatly saddened by the death of a loved one

mourn – to express grief

PHYSICAL SIDE EFFECTS

It had been six months since Desiree's dad died. Basketball season was starting soon, and her friends wanted her to try out for the team. But Desiree didn't feel like playing basketball. She didn't feel like doing anything. Ever since her father's death, she just wanted to be left alone and sleep. Her friends worried. Some thought it was time for her to get over it and move on. But Desiree's friend Lee lost his mom when he was younger. He knew Desiree just needed more time. He checked on her regularly and let her know he would always be available if she wanted to talk.

The way people deal with grief depends on their personality, age, culture, the type of loss they suffered, the circumstances surrounding the loss, and the support they receive. Although each loss is unique, many people share common physical side effects of grief.

While grieving, many people battle **fatigue**. Some will struggle with being able to sleep even though they may complain of exhaustion. Others may sleep in excess. Our bodies react differently to stress, but sleep problems are a common response.

Grief can cause physical pain. Some people experience headaches or other aches and pains. Others may feel a tightness in their chest or a shortness of breath. Although this can be scary, it is a common reaction to stress.

Some people lose their appetite and may struggle with digestive issues. Others may eat more than usual. When we suffer emotionally, our immune systems can weaken and make us more **susceptible** to illnesses. It is important to get proper nourishment when we mourn to help prevent sickness.

The Importance of Water

It's possible to become dehydrated while grieving. The bereaved can be distracted and confused and lack the energy it takes to care for themselves. Compound that with lots of crying, and there's potential for dehydration. Help those who are grieving by offering them water.

Grieving people often struggle to concentrate and complain of being forgetful. Fatigue, poor diet, and headaches make it difficult to focus. Although you may feel like you're losing your mind, in time this improves.

Although these physical symptoms can be uncomfortable and sometimes painful, they are natural. Don't judge yourself or consider yourself weak if you are experiencing some or all of these symptoms. Care for yourself and be patient with yourself as you wade through your grief.

Don't Hold Back

Sometimes, grieving people are told to be strong and not to cry. This is especially true for boys. Crying is healthy and healing. Don't be afraid to show your emotions with tears. Be true to your feelings and do what feels natural to you.

CHAPTER 3

COMMON REACTIONS

Cam's best friend in the world was his dog, Sampson. Every night for ten years, Sampson slept at the foot of Cam's bed. Then, Sampson got sick. The vet said there was nothing more they could do for him.

Cam was **furious**. He wanted a second opinion. He couldn't accept that his best friend was going to die. Cam yelled at his mom even though he knew it wasn't her fault. "I hate you all!" he screamed as he stormed out of the vet's exam room.

Many people experience feelings of anger when they grieve. Dr. Elisabeth Kübler-Ross identified these five common stages of grief: **denial**, anger, bargaining, **depression**, and acceptance.

Denial is typically the first reaction to grief. It is the brain's way of protecting us from feeling too much too fast. When you are in denial, you understand your loss, but you struggle to believe it.

Anger is a complicated emotion. You might be angry at the person who passed, the doctors, yourself, or the whole universe. Anger is natural, and can be healthy. No one should feel guilty for experiencing feelings of anger when dealing with loss.

In the bargaining stage of grief, you ask yourself *what if.* What if he had done something sooner? What if she had decided on a different treatment? What if you could trade places with your loved one? During this stage, you may cling to hope and relive the past instead of accepting what has happened.

Depression often occurs next. During depression, you become acutely aware of your pain. By working through depression, you begin to rebuild yourself and prepare for acceptance.

Super Sad? There's Help

Sometimes, you might feel alone and think that everyone is against you. You might experience low moods, which can lead to thoughts of self-harm or suicide. Always tell someone if you feel like harming yourself. Tell a trusted adult such as a parent, relative, teacher, clergy member, or medical professional who can help you get the support you need. The National Suicide Prevention Lifeline is available 24 hours a day to provide help at 1-800-273-8255.

The final stage of grief is acceptance. Acceptance does not mean being okay with your loss. Acceptance means finding a way to live with it. It requires growth, change, and time.

It's Normal to Repeat Yourself

When someone we love dies unexpectedly, we may feel compelled to tell the story of their death over and over again. This is normal! The more you share the story and circumstances of your loved one's death, the sooner you can begin to accept it.

Forgiveness helps heal a broken heart. When in mourning, forgive yourself for the things you said or did and for the things you wish you had said or done. Harboring **resentment** toward yourself makes remembering the good times more difficult.

Lend a Helping Hand

If someone you love has died from a disease, you might feel inspired to take action. Consider volunteering for an organization that raises money for medical research. You might want to participate in a fundraiser in honor of your loved one. Maybe you'll create your own organization to help fight the disease.

GRIEF RITUALS

It had been a year since Ramone died. The plaque in the schoolyard was covered with flowers, teddy bears, and balloons. The principal interrupted the morning announcements and asked for a moment of silence. Janelle watched as her teachers wiped their eyes and the atmosphere grew **somber**. Tears stung her eyes. Her chest felt tight. She missed her friend every day, but today was especially hard. Still, she didn't want to cry in front of her classmates. She didn't know how to act. Janelle wanted to go home and remember her friend in her own way in the privacy of her bedroom.

Grief **rituals** are ceremonial events meant to honor the deceased. They are often related to people's religious or spiritual beliefs and cultures. They can be public events such as funerals or other types of memorial services. These gatherings are opportunities for families and friends to come together and remember their loved ones. These ceremonies show respect to the person who has departed and provide comfort to those who remain.

Some people prefer to **memorialize** their loved ones with private rituals. They may remember their loved one in a way that is personal to them and their relationship. For example, you might return to a place that held special meaning to you and your loved one. You may listen to his favorite song or watch her favorite movie. Every relationship is unique and therefore the ways we remember the people we love will also be unique.

Although death is final, the bond we shared with our loved one doesn't have to end. We can continue to think and talk about them regularly, recall the advice they once gave, and relive the memories once shared. Your loved one will always be a part of you.

Write About It

If you are suffering from loss, consider journaling about your feelings. Journals are private and allow you to fully express your thoughts and emotions without concern for judgment. Journals are a great way to express grief. In time, you may look over past entries and realize how far you've come.

CHAPTER 5

LOOKING AHEAD

It had been three years since Alyssa's little sister passed away. Her family struggled for a long time, but they finally established a new normal. Her parents went back to work, and Alyssa was once more actively participating in school. Then one day, something Alyssa saw on TV reminded her of her sister. She felt the weight of her sorrow envelop her. Out of the blue, she was completely overcome with grief. Her pain felt as raw and new as it did on the day of her sister's death.

Sometimes, our loss is felt so deeply that we are forever changed. The more **traumatic** our loss, the more intense our pain. There is no time line for grief. Each person works through it at their own pace. Grief comes in waves, and sometimes it hits us at moments when we least expect it.

It's not surprising that holidays, birthdays, anniversaries, and special occasions often highlight our loved one's absence. It's helpful to prepare for these **momentous** occasions by creating a plan. Maybe surrounding yourself with family and friends and honoring traditions will help. Or maybe this is the year to break tradition and do something totally different. Planning for difficult days can help prepare us emotionally.

Sometimes, there are moments when grief catches us off guard. Maybe a certain smell triggers a memory. Or a song reminds us of the one we loved. These moments cannot be predicted, and the pain of loss can be staggering, regardless of how much time has passed. These unexpected moments of sadness can feel overwhelming. But eventually, they begin to decrease.

Sometimes, we need to take a break from our grief. Never hesitate to participate in enjoyable activities, such as watching a movie, spending time outdoors, or being with friends. Even while grieving, it is still okay to laugh and feel happy.

An Old Chinese Proverb

You cannot prevent the birds of sorrow from flying over your head, but you can prevent them from building nests in your hair.

CHAPTER 6

HELPING SOMEONE WHO IS GRIEVING

Kara and Alicia had been best friends since first grade. They did everything together. When Kara's mom got sick and died, Alicia didn't know how to talk to her best friend anymore. She worried she would say something to hurt Kara's feelings. She didn't want to talk about her mom and make her feel worse, so she avoided talking to Kara altogether. Kara didn't understand why Alicia was avoiding her. She thought she'd done something wrong. Alicia's behavior hurt Kara's feelings. Instead of losing one person she loved, she felt like she'd lost two.

It is difficult to know what to say to someone who is grieving. We often worry that we will upset the person by saying the wrong thing and cause more pain. One of the best things we can do for those who are grieving is to be a good listener. Don't try to force the bereaved into a conversation if they don't want to talk. Simply being present lets our loved ones know we are there for them. When the person seems ready, you can ask if they want to talk. If they do, listen and be compassionate. Don't give advice. Don't ask too many personal questions. Share your feelings, but don't compare your own grief to theirs.

Explain How You Feel

Has someone hurt your feelings while trying to comfort you in your grief? Maybe someone claimed to know how you feel. Or perhaps you've been told that because you're young, you'll get over it. Tell the person how their comments made you feel. Be honest but kind. Explain your feelings.

A grieving person may not feel comfortable asking for help. Instead of offering your assistance with questions like "Is there anything I can do for you?" be specific and intentional. For example, say, "I noticed you weren't in class today, so I took notes for you." Be helpful without waiting to be asked and without being **intrusive**. Most importantly, continue supporting your friend or loved one long after their loss.

Spend Some Time With Your Pet

Did you know that pets have healing powers? When petting your four-legged friend, you not only lower its pulse rate and blood pressure, but also your own. Animals offer many health benefits. Perhaps most importantly, they are nonjudgmental and love unconditionally.

Although grieving is painful and difficult, it can teach us to live more meaningful and richer lives. In order to get to a healthy place with our grief, we have to lean into it instead of avoiding it. We have to mourn, process, and eventually accept. Through loss and grief, we can learn to love more deeply, forgive more quickly, and appreciate each moment to its fullest.

Music Affects Our Moods

Music has the power to transport us. It can make us feel sad, lonely, happy, energized, peaceful, and hopeful. Take some time to explore different types of music and see which type fits your mood.

ACTIVITY

MAKE A MEMORY BOX

Memory boxes are wonderful ways to remember special moments in our lives and the ones we love. Find a box (a shoebox will work fine) and start by covering it with paper. A recycled paper bag works great! Cover the paper with drawings, words, stickers, and cut-outs. Make it unique, make it your own.

Fill the box with special memories of you and your loved one. Items can include old photographs, movie ticket stubs, letters, digital memorabilia, perfume or cologne, a piece of jewelry, an object, or anything that belonged to the one you loved and reminds you of what was special about them.

When you are ready, share the box with someone you trust. Take out each item and explain its significance. When you are feeling sad and missing your loved one, go through your memory box and remember all the happy moments you once shared.

GLOSSARY

denial (di-NYE-uhl): refusing to believe the truth

depression (di-PRESH-uhn): feelings of unhappiness that don't go away

fatigue (fuh-TEEG): feeling very tired or sleepy

furious (FYOOR-ee-uhs): extremely and intensely angry

intrusive (in-TROO-siv): characterized by interference that is uninvited and unwelcome

memorialize (muh-MOR-ee-uhl-ize): to remember someone or something

momentous (moh-MEN-tuhs): of great importance

resentment (ri-ZENT-ment): anger or displeasure that results from an insult, an injury, or an injustice

rituals (RICH-oo-uhls): actions or behaviors done in the same way repeatedly

somber (SAHM-bur): sad, dark, or depressed

susceptible (suh-SEP-tuh-buhl): vulnerable to being affected by something

traumatic (traw-MAT-ik): very shocking and upsetting

INDEX

acceptance 20, 23, 24
advice 30, 40
appetite 15
assistance 41
feelings 5, 6, 7, 17, 20, 21, 31, 39, 40
holidays 35
honor(ing) 25, 28, 35
memorial(ize) 28, 29
music 43
pain(ful) 5, 7, 14, 17, 23, 33, 34, 36, 40, 43
sleep 11, 13
stress 13, 14

TEXT-DEPENDENT QUESTIONS

1. What is the proper amount of time someone should be allowed to mourn?
2. What are some ways you can show support to someone who is grieving?
3. What are some of the physical side effects of grief?
4. List the five common stages of grief.
5. What are some ways we can keep memories of our loved one alive?

EXTENSION ACTIVITY

There are many ways people choose to honor their loved ones when they pass. Research grief rituals from various cultures and religions. Write about some of the ways people pay their last respects around the world.

BIBLIOGRAPHY

Axelrod, Julie. "The 5 Stages of Grief & Loss." *Psych Central.* psychcentral.com/lib/the-5-stages-of-loss-and-grief/. Accessed 25, Oct. 2018.

Belhumeur, Lorry Leigh. "How to Help Children Coping with Death, Loss, and Grief." *Western Youth Services (WYS).* www.westernyouthservices.org/children-coping-death-loss-grief/. Accessed 25, Oct. 2018.

Coleman, Paul. *Finding Peace When Your Heart Is in Pieces: A Step-by-Step Guide to the Other Side of Grief, Loss, and Pain.* Adams Media, 2014.

"Helping Grieving Children and Teenagers." Cancer.Net. www.cancer.net/coping-with-cancer/managing-emotions/grief-and-loss/helping-grieving-children-and-teenagers. Accessed 25, Oct. 2018.

James, W. John and Friedman, Russell. *The Grief Recovery Handbook.* Harper Collins, 2009.

James, W. John and Friedman, Russell. *When Children Grieve.* Harper Collins Publishers, 2001.

Kübler-Ross, Elisabeth and Kessler, David. *On Grief and Grieving.* Scribner, 2005.

Smith, Melinda, et al. "Coping with Grief and Loss." Coping with Grief and Loss: Dealing with the Grieving Process and Learning to Heal. www.helpguide.org/articles/grief/coping-with-grief-and-loss.htm. Accessed 25, Oct. 2018.

Smith, Melinda, et al. "Helping Someone Who's Grieving." Helping Someone Who's Grieving: What to Say and How to Comfort Others Through Bereavement, Grief, and Loss. www.helpguide.org/articles/grief/helping-someone-who-is-grieving.htm. Accessed 25, Oct. 2018.

Wolfelt, Alan D. *Healing Your Grieving Heart for Kids 100 Practical Ideas.* Companion Press, 2001.

Wolfelt, Alan D. *Healing Your Grieving Heart for Teens 100 Practical Ideas.* Companion Press, 2001.

About the Author

Michelle Garcia Andersen was an elementary teacher for many years. During the writing of this book, a dear friend from her school passed away unexpectedly. Michelle wishes to dedicate this book to Mr. Dan Dalton and to all of her friends at Hillside Elementary School. Mr. Dalton will be missed but never forgotten.

© 2020 Rourke Educational Media

All rights reserved. No part of this book may be reproduced or utilized in any form or by any means, electronic or mechanical including photocopying, recording, or by any information storage and retrieval system without permission in writing from the publisher.

www.rourkeeducationalmedia.com

PHOTO CREDITS: Cover:Top photo Shutterstock.com | Antonio Guillem, Bottom photo: Shutterstock.com | Diego Cervo Shutterstock.com, istock.com Page 4-5: istock.com | simonapilolla, istock.com | simonapilolla. Page 6-7: istock.com | Crazace2006, istock.com | bowdenimages. Page 8-9: istock.com | digitalskillet, istock.com | mactrunk. Page 10-11: istock.com | Wavebreakmedia, istock.com | davidford, istock.com | Wavebreakmedia. Page 12-13: istock.com | gpointstudio, stock.com | diego_cervo. Page 14-15: istock.com | smolaw11, istock.com | yacobchuk, istock.com | sonsam. Page 16-17: istock.com | DGLimages, istock.com | AndreaObzerova, istock.com | AntonioGuillem. Page 18-19: istock.com | Enjoyyourlife, istock. Com | Chalabala. Page 20-21: istock.com | seb_ra, istock.com | p_ponomareva, istock.com | AntonioGuillem. Page 22-23: istock.com | JochenSchoenfeld, istock.com | AntonioGuillem, istock.com | Srdjanns74. Page 24-25: istock.com | KatarzynaBialasiewicz, istock.com | GeorgeRudy, istock.com | mangostock. Page 26-27: istock.com | Dafinchi, Shutterstock.com | Monkey Business Images; Page 28-29: istock.com | Anze Furlan/psgtproductions, istock.com | Rawpixel, istock.com | demaerre. Page 30-31: istock.com | simonapilolla, istock.com | Alexlukin, istock.com | Maya23K. Page 32-33: istock.com | DragonImages, istock.com | DragonImages, istock.com | RyanKing999. Page 34-35: istock.com | bodnarchuk, istock.com | Kerkez. Page 36-37: istock.com | Yalana, istock.com | LightFieldStudios. Page 38-39: istock.com | Sladic, istock.com | Sladic. Page 40-41: istock.com | twinsterphoto, istock.com Elenathewise. Page 42-43: istock.com | Solovyova, istock.com | DGLimages.

Edited by: Kim Thompson

Produced by Blue Door Education for Rourke Educational Media. Cover and interior design by: Jennifer Dydyk

Library of Congress PCN Data

Coping With Loss and Grief / Michelle Garcia Andersen
(How to Deal)
ISBN 978-1-73161-488-9 (hard cover)
ISBN 978-1-73161-295-3 (soft cover)
ISBN 978-1-73161-593-0 (e-Book)
ISBN 978-1-73161-698-2 (e-Pub)
Library of Congress Control Number: 2019932313

Rourke Educational Media
Printed in the United States of America,
North Mankato, Minnesota